Magical Mystery Series
The Case of the Halloween Heist

Written By Brenda Elser & Kristin Loehrmann
Illustrated By Rose Mary Berlin

ACKNOWLEDGMENTS

From Brenda,

To my amazing husband, thank you for all of your support and confidence in me. You make my dreams come true every day! I'd also like to thank my parents for giving me some of their creative genius (lollypop trees still exist for me!). And to Kristin– Thank you for the humor and the beauty you add to our words when your write. Last (but not least - as the saying goes) I'd like to thank Nicholas Horcher for reading our work, you are a brilliant 11 year old Jr. Editor who is destined to go far!

From Kristin,

Thank you to my daughter Eva, who inspired the big words and big hair of "Eva" in the Magical Mystery Series. Thank you, also, to my father, for whom I attribute my attention to punctuation, as I still remember exactly the sentence he questioned when I wrote my first story at age eight. For the man in my life who helps me find my keys and brings me coffee in the mornings: my husband Eric; the encourager and believer who transcends all of my OCDs and obsessions. And for Brenda - the creative genius behind the series, who dreams in color and captures it all in words.

From both of us,

Thank you to our editor, Pamela Greenwood. Your feedback and questions spurred us on! A huge thank you to Rose Mary Berlin, our illustrator, who brought our words to life with her amazing artistic talent! We look forward to working with you both on the many more books in the Magical Mystery Series!!

Contents

1. The Note

It was a beautiful fall day just after Halloween – the kind of day that was cold when you stood in the shade, but when you stood in the sun it was too warm for a coat. The wind had a hint of more serious winter weather to come, and the trees had blanketed the ground with their colorful leaves.

Eva was in her front yard bundled up in a tan coat. As usual, she was liberally doused in color and wore a denim skirt and rainbow striped tights that matched her thin rainbow scarf. Over her tights she had added warm socks, one red and one blue, which now drooped around the top of her pink hiking boots. Her wild, strawberry blond curls fluttered about her face, teased by the gentle wind.

She'd finally finished piling the leaves into what she thought would be a big enough mound to jump in. This had been no easy task since the wind had worked equally hard at blowing them all away.

"Whew!" she huffed, as her pretty blue eyes examined her work. "That ought to last for at least two or three good jumps if I hurry!"

She stepped away from the pile to put the rake down, and turned to examine a nearby branch. She leaned her head to one side and put her hands on her hips as she looked up. *Was there a branch close enough for her to leap into the leaves from above?* she wondered when, quite suddenly, she felt someone rush past her shoulder followed by a loud war cry of "Whoop!"

Eva stood, her mouth open in amazement,

watching all of her carefully raked leaves scatter to the wind. Someone had just jumped into *her* leaf pile. "Someone stole my first leaf jump!" she fumed, clenching her hands at her sides. She didn't even need to see the head peeking out to know who that *someone* was.

"Robert!" she hollered, stomping one pink boot and shaking her fists in the air.

"Hey, Eva," he poked his tousled head up and grinned at her. Robert's short brown hair was usually messy so Eva didn't think anything of the twig that now stuck out from behind his ear. (He also generally wore the same mischievous grin that he was wearing now.) What pushed Eva's temper over the edge, though, was the look of fun in his brown eyes.

"Oh! I oughta! Oh! I'm gonna...." Eva sputtered dropping her fists and stomping toward Robert, who was buried up to his chin in *her* leaves.

"It wasn't my fault!" Robert laughed, scrambling around like a crab on all fours and dragging the back of his unzipped green coat though the leaves. "I was in such a hurry to get here and tell you something important that I couldn't stop fast enough... I... I tripped into your pile of leaves..."

"Gah!" Eva responded, yelling her own war cry and throwing her arms into the air, preparing to pounce on the leaf-jump thief (and perhaps make him eat a leaf or two), when she heard her name being called from across the yard.

"Eva! Oh, Eva! Wait! I have to talk to you! I have to tell you!" Lauren yelled running across the yard toward them, her purple coat flapping in the wind. She came to a breathless, jerky stop beside Eva and began talking before she could even catch her breath, "Eva... (pant) have you... (gulp)... checked your Halloween candy... (three more panting breaths then a single finger held up, asking them to give her a second.)... today?" There. She finally got it out.

Lauren was Eva's best friend; she was an adorable little blond who was a bit on the plump side. She was also the 'girly' type who usually dressed in coordinating outfits and liked things 'just so.' (She usually didn't run. It just wasn't ladylike. This explained why her dash across the yard seemed to have taken her breath away.)

Eva waited a moment to respond while she gave Robert the evil eye, which meant "I have not forgotten this," and let her friend finish catching her breath before she replied.

"No," she said, "My mom puts my Halloween candy in a cabinet in the kitchen. I only get a few pieces a day." In Eva's opinion, this was supremely unfair.

"Well, because it's," Lauren began, but Robert leapt up out of the remaining leaves and yelled, "*Yours* is gone too?" His sudden outburst caused Lauren to scream and spring straight into the air flailing her arms and legs.

"Geeze! Robert! Were you hiding there the whole time?" Lauren shouted, clutching her heart. "You practically scared the freckles right off my nose!" She crossed her arms and glared at him for good measure.

Eva and Robert both silently giggled and grinned at one another until Eva remembered she was mad at Robert too, and joined Lauren in giving him a good glare until he looked confused and shrugged at them both.

"Okay, okay," Eva said, mentally reminding herself to get back at Robert later for stealing her leaf jump. "What's up with your Halloween candy?" she asked, redirecting her friends to the more important topic.

"It's gone!" they shouted in unison.

With another quick glare at Robert, Lauren continued, "This morning after breakfast, I was going to count my stash again, but I discovered my candy was gone, and in its place was a note that saaaiiid...,"

Lauren drug the word out as she dug in her pocket for a piece of paper which she pulled out and read, "Dear Trick or Treater, sorry I had to snag your stash, but I'm down on luck and I needed some 'cash'. Better this doesn't rot the teeth out of your head, here's some floss for you instead. P.S. You will thank me later!

"Yes! I have exactly the same note!" Robert

said, pulling it from his pocket and holding it up along with a tube of dental floss.

Dear Trick or Treater,

Sorry I had to snag your stash, but I'm down on luck and needed some 'cash'.

Better this doesn't rot the teeth out of your head, here is some floss for you instead.

P.S. You'll thank me later!

"Well! I've called Brandon and Jenna and they have the exact same note *and* floss instead of their Halloween candy," Lauren said.

"You actually called Brandon Miller?" Eva blushed. "What did he say? What did he sound like? Did he ask about me?"

"Oh for cryin' out loud, Eva!" Robert rolled his eyes. "Brandon *said* he was missing his candy, of course. Geeze! Girls…" he muttered, shoving his hands into his pockets.

The three of them stood for a moment silently looking back and forth at one another. "Do you suppose *all* the children's Halloween candy *everywhere* was taken?" Eva whispered.

"Well," suggested Lauren, "maybe we should just check to see if yours is still there or if you have a note too. Let's go ask your mom."

With silent nods they all agreed and dashed around Eva's porch to the door that led into the mud room. Eva led the way into her kitchen where they found Mrs. O'Hare sitting at their old oak table watching the local news station on their small kitchen computer.

"Mom!" Eva began, but Mrs. O'Hare held up a hand telling them to stop and wait a moment.

"This just in!" the broadcaster announced in the way that broadcasters spoke which told you that what was "just in" was very important. "We are receiving reports from all across the town of Willows Heights that children's Halloween candy is missing. Thus far 88 concerned parents and their children have called the station to report that they woke up this morning with their candy stolen! A strange note and some dental floss were left in its place. Police have been notified but an active investigation has not been launched as it appears only candy has been taken. Could this be a prank by some strange criminal? Or, and this reporter must ask, have parents found a creative way to remove the Halloween candy from their children and get them to floss and brush instead? Details at eleven. This is Ted Tenesky reporting for Channel 7 news."

"My, oh my," Mrs. O'Hare whispered to herself, "Suspecting parents when it sounds so much like something Diva would do..."

"What, mom?"

"Sorry, nothing dear. Did you need me?" she

asked, smiling at them with a twinkle in her eye.

"Did you *hear* what the news guy said? The candy is gone in our whole town!" Robert crowed, pointing at the computer.

"You don't think parents would do such a thing, do you?" Lauren asked quietly, peeking under her lashes at Eva's mother.

"Mom," Eva interrupted her friends, "Can you get my Halloween candy down? We want to investigate the *crime* that has been committed!" Eva patted her pockets in search of the Junior Detective notebook she carried at all times as Robert and Lauren nodded behind her.

"Oh my, of course! What an excellent idea," Mrs. O'Hare said standing up and moving to the cupboard. There, she took down a very empty-looking bag. "Oh...yes. I'm afraid your candy is missing too, dear," she said shaking her head and holding out the bag for her daughter. Eva let out a squeak and rushed to grab her bag, only to find exactly the same note Lauren and Robert were now handing to her mother.

"Aww, mom! This is exactly why you should let me have more than a few pieces a day! I hardly got to eat *any* before this happened," Eva wailed.

"Now dear," her mother soothed her, rubbing her shoulder, "Don't worry. I'm sure with your great detective skills – and with the help of your friends – you'll find your missing candy in no time."

Eva felt a bit better hearing her mother's confidence in her and puffed out her chest. After all, she *had* read all of the Nancy Drew and Hardy Boy Detective novels, and she did have her Junior Detective field manual...

Of course they'd find the missing Halloween candy. Now the question was where to start?

2. Pumpkins Don't Talk

"So, ummm... Mrs. O'Hare? Any suggestions on what we should do first? To track down our stolen candy, I mean," Robert asked since the room had become very quiet.

"I was thinking!" Eva grumbled. She knew she should have suggested something right away - after all she was the lead detective in their group.

"Well, I have an idea," Mrs. O'Hare said absently, turning to the kitchen counter and looking through coupons. "We still have a Jack O 'Lantern on our front porch. If *anyone* will know where the Halloween candy has gone, it'll be him. Halloween lanterns know all sorts of things about Halloween! Why don't you go have a chat with him and see what he has to say?"

Now, Eva knew her mom was special and that she had some wild stories, but talking with a pumpkin? "Um, Mom, pumpkins don't talk," Eva said with an embarrassed glance at her friends.

"Yes, *pumpkins* don't talk, dear. But *Jack O 'Lanterns* do," she said, as if this were the most natural thing in the world. Then she gave a little laugh and a shake of her head. "The trick is getting them to talk about what you want to hear." She glanced up from the paper and into the children's confused eyes. "They aren't very smart, you know. I suppose it's from being hollowed out... empty heads and all... they tend to ramble."

"Mrs. O'Hare, are you saying that if we go out

to the front porch the Jack O 'Lantern will *talk* to us?" Lauren asked, tilting her head quizzically.

"Just go ask him, children. I'm sure he'll be happy to have someone listen to him for a change instead of ignoring him like we usually do." Mrs. O'Hare nodded with a smile before she turned to review her grocery list.

The children looked at one another with wide eyes, and with a collective shrug moved toward the front door.

"Oh! And one more thing, Eva," she called after them as they trailed out the kitchen and down the hall toward the front door. "When you're ready for him to stop talking just tell him to 'Hit the Road.'" She sang them the magic words, doing a little jig and playing an invisible guitar.

"How does she know all this stuff?" Robert whispered as they turned and walked down the hall to the front of the house.

Eva just smiled, "My family has some special connections. Mom says she'll tell me all about it someday."

They were almost out the front door when Eva heard her mother call one last thing from the kitchen. "Be inside before dark, young lady!"

"Aww, drat!" Eva mumbled shutting the front door behind her. What if they didn't solve the mystery before dark?

3. Fairy Dust

Eva was the last to tiptoe toward the Jack O' Lantern. The others were cautiously looking at it from a distance when she nudged her way closer to her friends' shoulders and whispered, "Has he said anything yet?"

Both Lauren and Robert silently shook their heads no. Each wore an expression of wonder, as if they thought the pumpkin was going to explode at any moment.

"You talk to it first," Robert whispered back. "It's your pumpkin."

Suddenly the pumpkin grinned, "Dude! I'm a Jack O' Lantern! Do I *look* like a pumpkin? I mean do ya see tha face? And by the way, isn't it ruuude for you to be talking about me like I'm not even here? I mean, what up with thaaa?"

"Ww...we...ell," Eva stuttered after a poke in the ribs from Lauren. "We certainly didn't mean to be rude. We haven't talked to a Jack O' Lantern before so..." And here the Jack O' Lantern cut her off.

"Ahh tha's cool. Hey! You can call me Jack. Sheaaahhh, it is so totally awesome to be, like, talking to people, you know? I, like, really need to be heard ya know? I mean I'm a Jack. I have feelings too. Hey, speaking of being heard - I *heard* that scream in the yard, little blonde chick! Dude, good scare!" he said, turning his pumpkin eyes toward Robert. "Now *that's* Halloween! Awesome, man, awesome. But it was, like, *not* cool how you stole little red-head chick's jump. Yeah! I saw that too and, like, that was *so not* Halloween."

"Wow. Pumpk... Jacks can talk fast," Lauren said turning to the others and whispering while the Jack continued holding its own conversation a short distance from them. "We're going to have to ask it a question quickly. What should we ask?"

"Well I think the obvious question is 'Where is our Halloween candy?'" Robert answered with a tone to his voice that said 'duh!'

"Like, was tha question directed at me, little dude?" Jack asked, suddenly breaking into their conversation. While the children had been huddled together they hadn't noticed the Jack O' Lantern seemed to have hopped his way over to join their little circle. "'Cause unlike some Jacks I can answer a question. I know we have a reputation for getting off topic and talking endlessly about... you know...whatever. Like my cousin, Jack the 50th, he was at this house down the street, but he talked nonstop until some teenager blew him up with a firecracker. I know, right? Totally uncool!" Jack's big jagged mouth twisted into a wobbly sideways S. "Can you believe thaaa? That is sooo not Halloween. Hey, speaking of..."

"Jack!" Eva interrupted, "Do you know where our Halloween candy is?"

"Wha?" he said, looking slightly stunned that his monologue had been halted. "Oh," he hopped away from them, "well sshheaaaahhh!"

"Well, don't crack your gourd or anything. Just tell us," Robert said.

"Ohhh so you think yer so smart, eh?" Jack said tilting his pumpkin head toward Robert. "Yer sooo smart but you can't even see the fairy dust that is, like, *all* around us? Dude, a fairy took the candy. Just follow the trail. Hey, that reminds me..."

"Jack!" Eva interrupted again. She now knew better than to let him get started. "What dust? We can't see any fairy dust."

"You can't?" Jack said, opening his triangle eyes even wider. "Weellp, let me shed some light on it for you." And with that the Jack O' Lantern began to glow. His face lit up gently at first, as if the candle had been relit inside his head, but slowly he began to glow brighter and brighter. The children turned away from the glare and squinted toward the yard, and as the Jack O' Lantern's light began to brighten outward, they *did* notice a sparkling trail had begun to appear.

"Oh, just look at it!" Lauren sighed. "It's so pretty! I can't believe we didn't see it before."

Floating in the air was a trail of sparkling rainbow-colored dust. It hovered in a bright path that lead from house to house, disappearing into the doors, windows, and chimneys of each home as far down the street as they could see. There was no doubt that this was a fairy trail.

"Whoooah..." Robert breathed. The children tiptoed down to the last step of Eva's porch looking further down the street at the rainbow path, while the Lantern rolled itself along the top of the porch following them. Jack stopped at the first step and opened his mouth when Robert and Eva abruptly sang, "Hit the Road!" and cut him off before he could say another word. The Jack twisted his expression into a pout and there he froze, once again a common Jack O' Lantern.

"Okay, let's do this quickly before our Jack Genius starts getting chatty again," Eva blurted. The other two nodded in agreement. They weren't sure how long the pumpkin would stay silent after they'd sung the magic words.

Eva hurriedly began to review their evidence, "We know a few things: Our candy is missing..."

"No duh," Robert interrupted.

Eva shot him a look and said, "A good detective lays out the facts." She continued, "Okay, our candy is missing, and we know that we all received the same note, *and* we know a fairy has been in all the houses."

"The fairy left us the note," Lauren said, coming to the obvious conclusion. The others nodded.

"Fairies aren't supposed to steal, are they?" Lauren asked with a catch in her voice. The tip of her nose began to turn red and her lower lip began to tremble. "I thought fairies were good," she whimpered.

"No, you're thinking of angels," Robert said walking up beside her and patting her shoulder. "Angels are good. Fairies...er.. well, fairies can be naughty. Not *bad* naughty. Just, well... playful naughty. You know?" Lauren nodded and sucked in her lower lip.

"I say we follow the trail right now and meet this scary fairy!" Eva said in a jesting tone to cheer her friend.

Lauren brightened at the rhyme and smiled a little. "Yeah. Let's meet this meany genie!" she added and they all giggled.

The mood had lightened and they were back to the adventure. Eva was eager to get started, but not about to be outdone in the rhyming game. "Yeah!" she almost shouted, "Let's meet this gobblin' goblin!" She slapped her knee and leaned over laughing. The others stood looking at her.

"Gobblin' goblin? Get it?" Eva tried again.

"I hope you are not saying our Halloween

candy has been gobbled!" Robert said, frowning. Lauren nodded behind him.

Eva opened her mouth to defend herself. (Really, why couldn't she say goblin when Lauren said genie? All magical creatures were fair game in this rhyming game, right?)

But her friends had already started running across the yard following the fairy trail. In the interest of solving the mystery *before* dark, she decided she would display her amazing grasp of the English language another time. Instead, she shrugged her shoulders, jumped off the step and ran after her friends.

4. One, Two, Thrrr....

The children followed the shimmery trail down the street past all of their houses; past the rusted mailbox shaped like a schoolhouse; past their bus stop; past the jungle gym with the huge tire swing; past the house with the red front door.

On the next block was the park, and there the rainbow stopped – which was a good thing since this was the farthest their mothers let them walk without adult supervision. The three children had been walking to this park (or had been pushed in strollers) for as long as any of them could remember. They knew every leaf on every tree of the park, so it seemed natural to Eva that if there was a clue to be found here, they were the best detectives for the job.

The children stopped side by side at the edge of the grounds. Each of them peered at the grass and trees but none of them was sure where to go now that the trail had stopped. The colorful dust seemed to linger in a cloud over the whole park.

Eva frowned and nodded her head, tapping her chin, as she was sure this was what all investigators learned in Detective School.

"What?" Robert said, nudging Eva and trying to see what it was she was nodding about. Lauren squinted into a nearby bush and poked at it with a stick she'd picked up.

"Do you see anyone?" she asked.

"Nope," Robert answered looking around

again. "Do you?"

"No!" Eva said triumphantly. "That's just it."

Now both Robert and Lauren were confused. "This is a park, and kids usually play here, right?" Eva asked, savoring the opportunity to show off her superior sleuthing skills.

They looked at her and Robert said, "Duh!" again.

Lauren giggled and tried to sound mysterious, "Sometimes – believe it or not – people even walk their dooogs here! Woooo-oo." She moaned and waved her hands up in the air as if she were a ghost herself.

"Hardy har," Eva said wrinkling her nose and taking her detective notebook out of her pocket so she could look official and in charge. "The park is empty and it looks like no one's been here for days. I don't even see any candy wrappers on the ground – and it's right after Halloween! That just isn't right. I know the fairy trail ends here but it feels like something's still *in* this park...and that something is probably scaring kids off. We should be careful."

With a nervous nod from Robert, the children edged farther into the park. No one voiced that they weren't exactly sure what it was they were looking for, but Eva was worried that Robert was going to find whatever it was first and seize the opportunity to be Mr. Smarty-Pants again.

As it turned out, Lauren found the first real clue. "Uh, you guys? Come over here!" Lauren shouted since Eva and Robert had spread out to opposite sides of the park. The two raced to where Lauren stood, trembling and looking quite pale. "Listen," was all she could squeak as they stopped next to her, becoming still.

Faintly above them they heard a slow, quiet moan, "Oooooooohhhhh. Geeeeeeze."

"Did someone just say 'Oh geeze'?" Eva whispered.

Lauren's green eyes had grown huge and she

trembled as she pointed straight up into the tallest oak tree.

The three of them looked up to see the branches quivering. One of the larger branches bowed as if it was supporting a great weight – but most surprising of all was the sight of a candy bag floating in midair. As they continued to stare, they saw pieces of candy being plucked by invisible hands and unwrapped. The candy disappeared into an invisible mouth while the wrappers floated down, along with leaves, to into a growing pile at the base of the tree below.

Eva whispered, "Something is up there." And if the three children weren't scared before, they certainly were now.

What person could climb a big oak tree like that without ropes or nets? The first limb was too high up for anyone to reach without that kind of help. At one time or another, every kid they knew had been dared to climb this enormous old tree. It was rumored to be haunted (after the school bully tossed little

Timmy Wilson's tennis shoe up into the tree hoping to lodge it in one of the branches, and the shoe had just disappeared).   No one actually believed the story, but the children tended to avoid the tree nevertheless.

"Well, who's gonna climb up there and check on it?" Robert asked.   Eva saw her friends looking at her as if to say 'You're the Junior Detective in charge!'

"Oh no, not me!" she said, quietly tucking her notebook back into her pocket.

"You've always said you were a stupid-ous climber," Robert said with a grin.

"Stu-PEN-dous climber!" said Eva, suddenly wondering whether now was the time to be bragging about her climbing abilities. "Anyway, I am not going up there – even if I *could* reach a branch.   Whoever is up there is just going to have to come down here!"   Even as she said it, Eva doubted this would really happen.

The three looked up again.   More leaves were

trickling down.

"Whoever… or *what*ever is up there might be able to tell us where our candy is," Lauren gulped.

Eva knew Lauren was right. She thought about all the effort she'd put into making her costume, and the fun time she'd spent going from house to house trick-or-treating… And she only got *a few measly* pieces! She grew angry thinking about all her candy being taken. And if *she* was mad, think about how the other kids felt!

"Alright you!" she shouted angrily up into the tree. The other two stepped back, surprised that she was suddenly yelling. They hadn't expected such a loud shout from someone who refused to take action just a second ago.

Lauren grabbed her hand in support. With more courage from her friends, Eva shouted again, "Yeah! You heard me! You get down here right now! And you better not even *think* about leaving!"

This was met with silence. The three children stared into the tree. There was no rustling, but they saw that no more leaves were dropping either. Eva began to despair. How could she convince this thief to come down and talk with them? She was much too mad to try a kinder approach. ("You catch more flies with honey than with vinegar," her mother always said.) So Eva did the only other thing she could think of; the only thing that had worked for generations. She brought out the secret weapon:

"Alright!" she said firmly, "I'm going to give you to the count of three!" She paused and saw the tree limbs tremble slightly.

"One!" A few quivering twigs fell.

"Twwooo!" she said louder and with a deeper voice. She thought she heard a yelp as the tree swayed slightly. "Don't make this any more difficult on yourself!" she shouted, buying time. She had never gotten to "Three" before. *No one* had ever gotten to Three as far as she knew. She lived in dread of hearing her parents say Three, so she never bothered to pursue whatever mischief she had currently been engaged in. But she knew whatever it was, Three was very, *very* bad.

There was a long pause, during which Eva gathered her courage, squeezed her eyes shut tight and said, "Thrrr..."

They heard a loud crack! Leaves and twigs began to fall from the tree in an avalanche. The children covered their heads to shelter themselves from the assault and fell to the ground. *Just my luck,* Eva thought, *I will be killed by an invisible something-er-other and no one will ever find my body.*

It was so unfair to not even have time to spell out 'WE TRIED TO SAVE THE CANDY' in fallen branches. At least then the newscaster could have told the town about the brave detectives. The local paper would have written a tribute to the heroes...

When the downpour stopped, the children peeped their heads up, shielding themselves in case there was another flurry. Carefully moving leaves and small branches aside, they stood and surveyed the damage. Mounds of wrappers and twigs were scattered around them and the base of the tree, making it nearly impossible for them to get to their feet. For a moment they were so engrossed in the piles that they didn't notice who brought the whole thing down.

5. Magic, people! Magic!

"Okay! Okaaay. Geesh," the voice above them said. The children looked up to find an enormously fat *ghost*. "You needn't be so cruel!" he sobbed, covering his face with transparent hands. "Don't you think *Three* is a little aggressive?" He shook so badly he seemed to fade in and out. Whoever this was had obviously gotten to Three before. *Maybe,* Eva thought, *three was what got him...here.* She gulped: *Dead!*

"Are you a *ghost*?" Robert asked cautiously.

"Of course I'm a ghost," sighed the spirit.

"Did you think I was the Easter Bunny? I mean, don't get me wrong. The Easter Bunny is very nice but you would *never* mistake me for him if you saw us together," he snorted.

He hovered just slightly above the rain of debris and reached into a small bag, pulling out a single piece of candy, which he tossed expertly into his mouth, wrapper and all. The three children stared at him with wide eyes. The ghost held the candy inside his closed mouth (which the children could see into since his cheeks and lips were milky sheer) and deftly unwrapped the treat with his ghostly tongue. He then blew out the wrapper in a puff through his pursed lips. Finally, he swallowed the now-unwrapped candy down his invisible throat into his very round belly where it bounced around and hung briefly like a fog. As the candy absorbed, the ghost appeared just a bit more solid and just a bit less transparent. The last remains of slimy candy dropped out through the wisp where his feet would have been, and it appeared to make the ghost feel better because he smiled and made quiet yummy noises to himself.

"Ohhh! Gross!" Eva exclaimed. Manners like chewing with your mouth closed didn't make much difference in this instance. There was really no way to avoid watching him eat like his mouth was open.

"Cool!" Robert crowed, jumping up and down, trying to indicate to the ghost that they should high five each other.

But it was Lauren the ghost faced and answered when she quaked, "Are you dead?"

"Sorry," the ghost exhaled sadly, "I eat when I'm depressed... and I wouldn't exactly say 'dead.'"

"But not exactly alive either," Lauren whispered with a shudder.

"Were you born a ghost?" Robert interrupted. Eva was beginning to be embarrassed for them. She didn't know much about ghosts either, but she certainly didn't want the *ghost* to know that. How were they going to maintain an air of authority as detectives if they were so obviously confused?

The ghost ignored them and said wistfully to himself, "They just keep making candy better and better... In my day, all we had was horehound and molasses chews..." Eva didn't know what horehound was, but it sounded like some kind of scary dog that guarded the swampy marshlands of a haunted burial ground.

"Horehound. Yeah. Terrible stuff," Robert said, nodding and acting as if he knew just what the ghost meant. He turned to the girls and shrugged.

Eva took control of the situation once again. "How is it you came to be in possession of that piece of candy? Where is the rest of it?" she demanded shaking her finger at the ghost.

"Oh, I didn't take it, if that's what you mean," the ghost said sorrowfully.

Eva sputtered, "Well if you didn't take it, how did you *get* it?"

"Yeah!" Robert said, putting his hands on his hips and glaring at the ghost, "And you still didn't answer my question: Were you born a ghost?"

Eva whispered, "Robert! That is not important right now! Do you want to get to the bottom of this mystery and get our candy back or not?" Robert looked uncomfortable. Eva turned to Lauren for support, but saw that Lauren was still frozen. She could not seem to take her eyes off the ghost. Nor could she seem to fully close her mouth.

"I was not born a ghost, and Diva gave it to me," the ghost answered twisting his hands together and making them look like a twisted towel being wrung out. "Ooooohhh...be nice to me. I'm under a lot of stress right now," he cried, as rolls of misty fat seemed to droop further down.

"Whaa?" said Eva. "What's the matter? Who is Diva?"

Robert asked at the same time, "What *were* you once?"

"Is this some kind of cruel game?" the ghost hiccupped. "Okay, the Tooth Fairy, of course, and I was once a dentist."

Now the children were thoroughly confused. They stared at the ghost who slowly wobbled and sagged before them.

"Diva is the Tooth Fairy?" Eva asked, changing the tactic to 'good cop' and using a gentle tone with the depressed ghost.

"Yes, she is one of the many tooth fairies employed by the Tooth Corporation." he warbled in a watery moan. "And I was once a dentist. My great grandfather was a dentist. My grandfather was a dentist. My father, uncles and brothers were all dentists. I had no choice." The ghost moaned again. Eva noted that while this ghost was massive and could probably do a lot to scare people, he was just too forlorn to get the job done.

Finally Lauren spoke. "Oh...my...gosh..." They turned to stare at her.

The ghost hung his head, ashamed. "I wanted

to be a librarian."

"And Diva?" Eva said, ignoring Lauren for the moment, and trying to get them all back on track, "The Tooth Fairy. *She* gave you that piece of candy?"

"Yes," said the ghost with his eyes still downcast.

"Why?" asked Robert.

"Because," sighed the ghost, "I was her personal trainer and she paid me in candy. All Halloween spirits are paid in candy. That's our form of money." He sobbed pointing to the wrapper, "That was my very last piece!"

"*You're* some kind of fitness instructor?" Eva asked with one eyebrow raised.

The ghost nodded at her and insisted, "I *was* a fitness instructor! She had to lay me off. Diva's in a bad financial situation right now," he explained in her defense. "She had to use your candy to pay for the debt she's in."

"The Tooth Fairy's in debt?" Lauren whispered. "You mean because of inflation? Because I remember when I used to get a quarter for losing a tooth, and then it went up to a dollar." The children nodded in agreement.

"No, not inflation," said the ghost, and then shut his mouth uncomfortably. "I shouldn't talk about this," he mumbled literally folding his lips. "Mima Mumsent mant me moo malk mumout mer mivet mismess."

Eva (who spoke fluent Lip Fold) interpreted this to mean "Diva doesn't want me to talk about her private business." She turned back to the ghost and urged him to share more information, "But this note..." she dug the piece of paper out of her pocket and read, "Dear Trick or Treater, sorry I had to snag your stash, But I'm down on luck and I needed some 'cash'. Better this doesn't rot the teeth out of your head, here's some floss for you instead. P.S. You will thank me later!"

"Did you like that?" the ghost asked

unfolding his lips and giving them a small grin. He seemed to brighten a bit and he looked pleased with himself. "I suggested she add the part about the dental floss." He bragged opening his mouth in a wide toothless grin. Even if he was a ghost it was easy for the children to see that he had no teeth. "You really should take care of your teeth," he said. "But then, you probably already know that." He shut his mouth, becoming serious again.

"Is that what killed you?" Robert asked cautiously.

"You could say that," sighed the ghost. "I died of an infection... A little boy came into the office with a nasty cavity. When I tried to check the tooth, he bit off my finger." The ghost held up his ghoulish hand. Indeed there was a missing index finger. "The infection set in so quickly there was no time to treat me," he moaned. "I died within the week."

The children went to comfort him. Robert

patted the ghost's tail (which, of course meant he was patting the air). Eva reached for his ghostly hand but only grabbed a leaf the ghost had been holding. Lauren simply said, "Oh, I'm so sorry," and quietly stepped farther away.

He seemed to respond to their kindness and moaned harder sharing his plight with them, "Now I'm not a dentist *or* Diva's personal trainer. I'm not sure what I'm going to do for Halloween candy." If ghosts could cry, this ghost looked like he was going to. "Diva's in a bad situation," he repeated. "But she gave me a job, and she's the only real friend I have... If I don't get a job I will simply die. *Again!* Just look at me! I'm wasting away!" He held his arms out for them to better observe his robust figure. "Do you know how long it's been since I've had a regular Halloween candy-paying job?" he sobbed.

Eva didn't know whether to feel bad for the Tooth Fairy, or remain angry that their candy had been stolen. She didn't care what kind of "situation" the Tooth Fairy was in. Stealing was wrong. Still, she did feel bad for the ghost.

"Okay, okay, let me just get this straight," she said in her best detective voice. "Normally Diva pays her employees in candy, because that's what Halloween spirits use for money, but she can't afford to buy any candy to pay them with, so she stole ours? Did I get that right?"

"Well, when you say it like *that*," the ghost sniffed, "it sounds so criminal!"

"Really! Criminal, huh?" Lauren yelled, finally finding her voice and startling everyone. "Criminal is when you take something that is not yours and you don't ask for it. It is also called stealing, in case there was any confusion!"

The ghost just sobbed louder, and Eva was secretly pleased that now there was a 'bad cop' to this game. "Now hang on here," she said, shooting Lauren a congratulatory smile. "She took, stole, what-ever-ed our Halloween candy to pay the spirits. But normally she'd just *buy* the candy, right? I mean, she must have an endless supply of coins."

"No," the ghost said, as if it should be obvious. "Honestly, don't they teach you *anything* about magical creatures in school? The Tooth Corporation allows a budget of coins to each Tooth Fairy to leave under children's pillows in their Territory."

"Tooth Fairies work for a place called the Tooth Corporation? Well, don't they pay Diva? Why does she have to take candy?" Eva asked.

"Of course she gets paid...It's just not enough and Tooth Corporation coins are ONLY for children who leave their teeth under their pillows. After all, fairies can't stop giving children coins or the children will stop believing in them and stop leaving their teeth," he explained.

The children all stood looking at the ghost with amazement.

"You honestly didn't know any of this?"

"No," Robert said with a slight scowl, "and I am gonna say something to my teacher because this is *way* more interesting than math!"

"What does the Tooth Corporation do with the baby teeth?" Lauren asked.

"Oh my goodness!" huffed the surprised ghost. "Baby teeth can be used for wishes, of course! Once you have enough of them in the bank anyone can do some really big magic! How do they explain how rockets get to the moon in this..." he paused to make ghostly quote marks, *'school'* of yours? I mean without magic, those huge hunks of metal would never make it off the ground!"

The children practically spoke at once when the ghost was finished. "Oh my gosh!" Robert exclaimed, jumping up and down. "I have a loose tooth right now! I'm gonna wish for that bike I want! No wait, I'm gonna wish to be a kajillionaire! No wait...I'm gonna wish for a kajillion wishes and *then* I'm gonna wish for my bike. My parents are going to be so happy!" he hollered, leaping into the air over and over again and flailing his arms and legs.

"I have a loose tooth too!" Eva said with a smile as she reached up and wiggled her front tooth to show her friends. "Are front teeth worth bigger wishes?" she asked, turning to the ghost.

Lauren rolled her eyes and said, "That is just crazy talk. If baby teeth could give people wishes no one would give their teeth to the Tooth Fairy. We would all keep our teeth and make our own wishes."

"The wishes don't work like that in *your* land, silly children!" he explained, waving his hands to indicate they should calm down. "They work in Fairy Land and the Tooth Corporation refines them into a *special* magic to sell back to your world. Even in Fairy land you can't just *have* a baby tooth. We can't have everyone walking around with a huge supply of wishes! Can you imagine the chaos? We'd be tripping over bikes and toys and candy everywhere! It would ruin our economy... That's why there are Tooth Fairies! They collect all the baby teeth, and the Tooth Corporation invests the teeth and collects all the magic. They contract out the wishes to places like NASA so your world can do things like fly. Or talk to each other from really far distances. Geeze, you didn't think those tiny little boxes you call phones actually allowed you to hear other people's voices from across the country did you? Magic, people! Magic!"

The children stared at him silently now, expressions of surprise and disappointment on their faces.

"Drat!" Robert finally moaned dropping his arms and slouching as though his world was ending.

"No way!" Lauren added, so caught up in the conversation she forgot to be scared of the ghost at all anymore.

Eva sighed and stopped wiggling her tooth. "Okay, this has all been very... educational,

Mr. Ghost. Thank you for sharing. But I think we should focus on finding our candy now," Eva said, trying to bring everyone back on track. "Do you think you could bring us to this Tooth Fairy, er... Ms. Diva, so we can talk with her?"

"Yeah," Lauren nodded, quickly remembering the mission. "Maybe we can work something out that would solve everyone's problem!"

"How would you solve everyone's problem?" the ghost asked with a sniff. "You clearly don't even know anything about Fairy Land."

"Uh..." Eva stalled. "Let me discuss this with my associates." She pulled the children further away and looked at them seriously. "What should we do?" she asked.

"I, for one, am having a very hard time believing this," Lauren said skeptically.

"I know!" Robert added. "He is a personal trainer? Come *on*. How realistic is that?"

The girls stared at him. Maybe it shouldn't

have surprise them that he'd focused on the ghost's job rather than what they just learned about baby teeth, wishes, and the Tooth Fairy...but it did. Robert continued, "What! He's huge! Would *you* hire a personal trainer like that?"

"I have an idea," Eva said, ignoring Robert and giving her friends a big smile and a wink as she pulled away from their huddle. "Mr. Ghost, we may not know a lot about Fairy Land but we do have something the Tooth Fairy could use: Our baby teeth! Since Robert and I have loose teeth, maybe we could offer them to Diva as payment for our candy. And *she* could use the wishes instead of bringing them to the Tooth Corporation. I mean the teeth are ours to offer as payment, right?"

"Hey! My tooth isn't ready to come out yet! " Robert exclaimed.

"Robert, would you rather have your Halloween candy or a measly coin? I'm sure you could work it loose by the time we get to the Tooth Fairy's house." Eva turned her back on the ghost and winked repeatedly at him.

"What's wrong with your eye, Eva? Are you flirting with me? I thought you liked Brandon Miller?" he looked confused.

Lauren pushed his shoulder gently and leaned over to whisper in his ear, "You might not have to give her your tooth, Robert. We just need to get to Fairy Land."

"Ohh... Right!" he yelled. "Sure, she can have my loose tooth!" He nodded, blinking both eyes at the girls and looking as though he had developed a strange twitch.

Eva glared at him and shook her head, but the ghost didn't seem to notice the boy's odd behavior. He looked thoughtful and a little brighter. "I guess Diva wouldn't mind if I brought you to her for that. Like you said, maybe you could offer your teeth to *her* as wish payment!" The children assured him they had only good intentions. He began to float closer to where they stood.

"Why," Lauren suddenly asked watching the

ghost come closer, "would the Tooth Fairy hire Halloween spirits in the first place?"

The ghost looked thoughtful. "That is a great question, young lady. Come closer and I'll show you more..."

6. Diva's House

The children huddled closer to the ghost looming in the center of them. He spoke quietly and with great emotion. Anyone who may have been watching from a distance would have wondered what three children in a park were doing standing in a loose circle, nodding periodically to themselves. To the distant eye, the ghost did not exist. His shadowy presence could only be seen up close, and his voice could only be heard by the children.

"Come a little closer," he said, "You! Little blond girl. You must come closer."

Lauren reluctantly shuffled her way closer to the ghost and his gelatinous arms reached out to surround the three of them as if he were about to give them a big hug. Suddenly, the children felt themselves being pulled toward his belly like they were being sucked in by a vacuum. "Hold on!" they heard him cry as the draw intensified.

Lauren began screaming for all she was worth (or was that Robert?) as they were drawn down into a tunnel.

This feels like a water slide, Eva thought as she whooped and turned in the slippery spiral of the long glowing tunnel. "Oh - my scarf!" she cried reaching for it as it flew from her shoulders, spinning just out of reach.

But just as abruptly as it had begun, the ride ended and she was dumped out onto lush green grass. A second later she heard a 'whump,' and Robert landed on the grass next to her.

Having already been almost squashed by one friend, Eva deduced that the screams coming from above them belonged to Lauren, and she had just enough time to grab Robert's hand so she could yank him aside. They looked up and saw Lauren slide out of a huge green and orange pumpkin vine which appeared out of nowhere and hovered above them in the sky.

Lauren landed face down in the springy grass and rolled twice, still screaming, which resulted in a mouth full of sod.

Both Robert and Eva rushed to her side when the ghost reappeared behind them. "Ta-daaa!" he exclaimed holding his arms out to both sides and giving them a small bow along with his toothless smile.

"What have you done?" Eva asked, kneeling beside her quivering friend and putting her arms around her. "Where are we?"

"Well, we're in Fairy Land, of course! Where did you expect the Tooth Fairy to live?" He looked disappointed that the ride they'd just taken was not as appreciated as he thought it would be.

Lauren began to howl, "We slid down a ghost's intestines! Augh!! I'm gonna be sick!!"

Eva turned back and glared at their mode of transport. "Ewww! Double gross!"

"Dude! Is *that* what that slidey thing was?"

Robert shouted. "Oh, man! That's gross even for me! I think I'm gonna hurl!"

The ghost huffed, "That was *not* my intestines! Where did you get that idea? That was a *vine* from the Great Halloween Pumpkin. You can take the vines anywhere from September to December. They're like trains for Halloween spirits."

Eva made a mental note of this for later, and Lauren seemed to calm down a little after hearing this. She sat up, spitting grass, and said, "I'm not supposed to go places with strangers."

"After all that, you still call me a stranger?" the ghost asked. "Well, allow me to introduce myself then," he said, "I'm Dr. Stubben – but you can call me Stubby for short...everyone else does."

"Heh," Robert giggled, "Stubby? That's a funny nickname!"

"Yeah, Funny!" Eva said recovering a bit and helping Lauren stand up. "Well, I'm Eva," she introduced herself, "and this is Lauren, and that's Robert."

"Nice to be formally introduced. Better late than never I say!" Stubby said to the children with another awkward little bow.

"Wait. We are in *actual* Fairy Land?" Robert said. The ghost only smiled, looking pleased at the children's amazement.

It appeared to be twilight and there were gentle stars just visible in the colorful sunset. The air was filled with the scent of flowers and everywhere they looked the greenery was carefully landscaped. The bushes were beautifully pruned and designed into patterns or topiaries. The grass was lush and green, sculpted, edged, and cut in pretty patterns. Each flower bed seemed to be carefully designed for the perfect color combinations. The children could see they were in a small park near a cul-de-sac of lovely, expensive-looking homes. Several of them looked brand new or as if they were being remodeled. This appeared to be a very rich and fashionable neighborhood.

"I did not picture Fairy Land as having neighborhoods," Eva commented. "And I thought they were supposed to be tiny."

"Well, we are *all* tiny now, of course. The Halloween Vine made us the right size for our destination. Seriously, you children have a real gap in your education! I mean, how did you think Fairies lived?"

"Um... I guess I thought they lived under flower petals or in trees," Eva answered hesitantly. Lauren nodded in agreement.

"Clearly..." Stubby snorted, "You have not met any Fairies!" When they continued to look doubtful he explained, "Fairies have a real sense of fashion and style. Not just their clothes, mind you, but their homes! It's really hard to get featured in the magazine 'Fairy House Beautiful' around here because the competition is so tough," he sighed. "And their clothes... Oh, and their shoes! I mean, don't even bother walking out of the house holding your head up if you're wearing the wrong shoes! It is *the* faux pas – if you're a Fairy, of course," he added, looking down at his own ghostly tail.

"Okaaay," Robert said, looking a little disturbed. "Maybe we should just head over to the Tooth Fairy's house and not plan any uninvited tours of Fairy homes."

Both of the girls examined their grass-stained clothes and sloppy boots. After the short trip down the Halloween vine Eva's hair was now a tangled, curly mass standing out around her head. They agreed with Robert. They would head directly to the Tooth Fairy's house.

"Fine with me," Stubby said, still miffed that the vine ride had not been appreciated.

He turned in a few ghostly circles. "Just getting my bearings," he reassured them. Finally he began drifting toward a wide street corner with a lovely sign on it engraved with the name Sugar Plum Ave. "This way!" he called back to them.

"So... I was wondering," Stubby mused

while they walked, "When you talk with Diva would you mind asking her if I could have my old job back? Perhaps you could tell her I was once *your* personal trainer? Oop, wait!" He interrupted his own thought. "We needed to take the street we just passed." He turned the group around again.

"I guess," Robert answered, looking at the girls. "I don't think it would do any harm. But just so we're clear, you're referring to physical fitness? Seriously?"

Lauren, who seemed to be doing better since she was 'ohhh-ing and ahhh-ing' over the beautiful homes in the neighborhood, shot a look at Robert.

Eva pointed out the carefully manicured tree on the house in front of them with the bushes pruned to look like grazing unicorns in the lawn, "It's like we're walking through the pages of some magazine," she grinned, "Everything is *so* beautiful. Like a better version of the multi-million dollar neighborhood my parents once drove me through."

"Yeah it's weird," Robert said.

"I like it," Lauren giggled.

"Ooops, wrong way again..." Stubby laughed looking nervous. "All these expensive neighborhoods look alike to me."

After another couple of backtracks Eva finally stopped. "You're *lost*," she announced, pointing her finger at the ghost and shaking it.

"What?!" Stubby said turning around. "I most certainly am not!"

"You are!" Eva insisted. "Where is everyone? Why don't you just ask for directions?" she demanded. "Here's someone coming now. Excuse me, Excuse me sir!" When the man was close enough to see, Eva gasped. There, floating in the air slightly above the sidewalk, flitted the most beautiful man she had ever seen. He paused to raise an eyebrow at the spectacle of grubby children - and one confused ghost. With shining blue, butterfly wings, he was dressed for an evening out in a tailored gray suit and a blue silk tie that exactly matched the blue in his wings. His hair was carefully groomed and sparkled with golden highlights. His sideburns were sculpted to enhance his high cheekbones and handsome features... And his *shoes*!

Eva immediately felt self-conscious.

"I do not need directions, thank you very much!" Stubby insisted, avoiding the eyes of the elegant man.

"*Clearly* you do," the Fairy replied with a sniff, looking at the rumpled bunch. He raised his eyebrow at them and held a delicate handkerchief in front of his mouth and nose.

"Well!" Lauren said, "There's no need to be rude!"

"I wouldn't dream of being rude, girlfriend," he said with a wink and a grin, getting serious and swishing his wings, "It's not fashionable. Now... What exactly can I do for you?" he asked, brushing invisible specks from his exquisite jacket.

"Can you point us in the direction of the Tooth Fairy's house?" Robert asked.

"Can I!" he said with a snap. "It's right over there!" He turned in a perfect arabesque and pointed toward a much larger structure off in the distance which could clearly be seen from where they were standing. "I wouldn't go there if I were you, though," he added with a dramatic wave. "She's having some *much-*needed work done on her house and it's just not ready yet. The Cavity Creepers *alone* have not been... well... *exterminated*," he said lowering his voice as if it was embarrassing to discuss. "Between you and me, I'm surprised the Homeowners' Association let it get that bad. Some people!" He stopped suddenly, looking embarrassed at his outburst, and glanced at his expensive watch, "I'm so sorry, whoever you are, but I must fly! I'm off to join the others at the Governor's Ball and I'm late... Fashionably late, of course. Ta-taaaa!" Then he winked again and flew off in a rainbow of glitter.

"Oh, he was so pretty," Lauren murmured.

"No way!" Eva fumed turning to their ghostly guide. "It was right there all along and you have been leading us in circles?"

"Welll... I thooouuught that house *did* look familiar. She's done an awful lot of remodeling," he said defensively.

"Fine. Don't go into a meltdown," Eva huffed. Literally – his chubby tummy was beginning to look droopy again. "Let's just go," she said angrily. She had no idea what time it was, but certainly this bumbling around was eating into their time before it grew dark.

Four short blocks later they stood at the front lawn of the Tooth Fairy's house. Eva felt bad for yelling at Stubby as she stood in front of the home. *How come we didn't recognize it?* she thought to herself. *It looks like an upside-down tooth!*

And it did. The outside was smooth and shiny white. There were no windows and the walls curved to make the home an oval shape. Pointy root-like peaks made up the roof and these had lovely caps and flags mounted on the tips making them look like the towers of a castle.

The four of them approached a fancy front door which appeared to be the only opening to the home. When no one else moved, Eva knocked. Robert began examining the exterior walls of the house. Stubby seemed to be concentrating on keeping his tummy sucked in, and Lauren was looking uncertain again.

A regal-looking ghost answered the door, but before any of them could say a word he droned, "The servant's entrance is around the back."

"I'm sorry, but we're actually here to see the Tooth, uh, Mrs., I mean Ms... We're here to see Diva," Eva blurted before the ghost butler could close the door.

"I see," the ghost butler moaned opening the door further and eyeing Stubby suspiciously. "Well, come in then. Ms. Tooth has not taken many visitors since the reconstruction began." The ghost butler gestured for them to enter.

The interior hallway of the tooth home was swarming with supernatural workers who were scrubbing the walls with giant toothbrushes. Everywhere the spirits had already scrubbed, the walls were white and shiny like a freshly-cleaned tooth. The walls they had not yet worked on looked yellow and dingy. Darker spots could even been seen in the corners and across the floor. These areas were marked with red tape and cones to keep others away.

"Please excuse the mess," the butler groaned as he led them past a grand curved stairwell to a room on the right. "We are remodeling as you can see. Is Ms. Tooth expecting you?"

The four looked at each other guiltily.

"Not exactly," Eva said when Lauren nudged her. "But I'm sure she'll want to see us once she hears what we have to offer."

The butler sniffed, "Wait here and I will let Ms. Tooth know she has, ahem... *visitors*." He paused and turned to Stubby, "I am certain you understand how busy she is," he said shutting the door, leaving them in the grand sitting room.

The room looked as though it had been completely refinished. Everything in it was a pristine white. White couches faced one another with a white coffee table in between. The walls were so smooth and white they *actually* glowed. There were fancy white chairs in front of the lovely white curtains that framed a glimmering wall.

The group stayed huddled together in the spot the butler had left them, looking around the room, not stepping anywhere.

"Gosh," Eva finally breathed, "I'm afraid to move and get anything dirty."

"Hey," Robert turned to Lauren, "How do my teeth look? I think I forgot to brush them this morning. Do you think the Tooth Fairy will notice?" He opened his mouth wide.

"Like you ever brush your teeth," Eva interrupted. "Did you guys notice there are no windows in this place?"

The children looked around the room and Stubby opened his mouth to explain when the white door opened and Diva entered as if on cue.

7. Freeeze!

She glided across the floor like an elegant dancer, looking directly at each of the children as she passed. Her first words were to Robert, "Young man," she said, "*you* did not brush your teeth this morning. Eva and Lauren, show me your teeth as well!" She sniffed. "Just as I thought... Barely brushed – and none of you flossed." Here she gave a dramatic sigh. "Don't bother trying to deny it. I'm your Tooth Fairy. You cannot hide these things from me." Robert quickly clamped his lips together.

Diva raised a well-shaped brow and pursed her perfectly pink frosted lips at him. She was, of course, dressed head to dainty toe in white. Then she looked at Stubby, whose eyes were busily looking at his tail. "Well, long time no see," she said to him. "I see you didn't make your severance pay last very long," she sniffed.

"She looks like she's ready for a fancy evening on the town or something," Eva whispered to Lauren. Diva was tall and wore a long glittering white mermaid-style evening dress, though it was a bit too tight for her slightly plump figure. Her white hair was piled very high on top of her head with pin-curls falling around her face. Her makeup was obviously carefully done, and she had on long white gloves to complete her outfit.

"Oh..." Lauren whispered, "You look like a bride."

This innocent comment seemed to annoy Diva because her lips turned downward and she stopped looking at the squirming ghost to turn her gaze on the rest of the group.

"Well!" she seethed, turning her back and walking farther into the room so they could now see the large silver wings that were folded and laying down her back. "I am dressed for the ball tonight. I've never, *never* been mistaken for a human before... Are these the manners your mothers taught you? You meet someone for the first time and you insult them?" She folded her arms and glared at them from across the room. "What are you doing here anyway? I don't allow children in my home. Leave at once." She demanded with a snap when Stubby suddenly spoke.

"These kids had an idea, Diva. It *could* just solve all your, er, *our* problems." He gulped and continued nervously, "They have loose baby teeth you could use to finish your home remodel... Maybe even hire a few employees back?" he squeaked out the very last part since Diva had curled her lip at him and was clenching a fist.

"My *dear* Dr. Stubben, you *know* that Tooth Fairies cannot steal baby teeth from the Tooth Corporation. The Corporation would know instantly and the Tooth Fairy would be banished from Fairy Land forever! Are you trying to get me banished, hmmm?" she sneered, slowly walking toward them.

"No, no! Of course not," the ghost moaned. He had begun to look a bit fuzzy around the edges and Eva didn't think he had much more in him so she spoke up.

"We thought maybe we could strike a little deal with you. The baby teeth are ours to give away, so we thought if we gave them to you *personally* you could give us back our Halloween candy. This way everyone gets what they need."

"Oh, you think *I* have your Halloween candy, hm? I wonder who could have told you that…" she said with another glare at Stubby. In a moment she stepped back and her expression became thoughtful. "Let me check on this," she mumbled and sharply clapped her hands together twice.

Instantly, with a silvery poof, a delicate pair of silver rhinestone-rimmed glasses appeared on her nose and a scroll floated in front of her. She reached out and began to unroll it, reading parts out loud every once in awhile:

"…The Party herein, blah, blah, blah… Who-in agrees to amass aforementioned Baby Teeth for The Tooth Corporation herein going forward known as The Party of the First Part, blah, blah, blah… Ah! Here it is!" She grew very quiet as she scanned the document.

Finally she turned around to face her uninvited guests. Diva had an evil smile that did not make the children feel any better. "Well! I must say, aren't you clever little children catching that little loophole in the contract." She crooned, "What did you say your names were again?"

But before anyone could remind her that she'd already embarrassed them by name she continued, "Not that it matters. We will have plenty of time to get to know one another during your stay here."

"Excuse me?" Eva jumped in, "Thank you for the offer to let us stay in your, uh, very, uh sparkly... castle, er, tooth home... but I have to be back before dark so perhaps we could just collect our candy, sign a contract or something and give you one of our teeth when they come out? Then we'll just be on our way."

"Oh no, dear children! I insist that you stay!" she said with a sneer, and sharply clapped her hands again. "Now that you have pointed out the obvious *oversight* in the contract, it has become clear that I am entitled to several baby teeth - *given* to me - and the Tooth Corporation will have nothing to say about it because the teeth were not collected under pillows or within special tooth boxes. I will *graciously* allow the children of the world to give me their baby teeth in exchange for their precious Halloween candy *every year*!"

The doors suddenly flew open with a loud bang and in rushed six very nasty-looking guards. Some seemed to be made up of rotten food with corn cob noses and moldy cookie crumb eyes, while others looked as if they were composed of damp towels and wrinkled clothes that had been left on the floor too long. Eva noted that they each wore little white booties on their feet to keep the floors clean. The moldy men all wore black uniforms and had a sharp pick-like instrument attached to their belts. They were dripping slime, and furry white lumps were growing on several parts of them. Worst of all - they smelled *terrible*. In each guard's moldy green hand, a length of flossy rope was held at the ready.

"Eeewww! What are those?" Lauren shrieked.

Diva's brittle laugh bounced across the shiny floor and echoed along the walls. "Those are the Rot Guards, my dears," she snickered. "Don't you ever wonder what happens to things that are left for too long? First, they rot. *Then they come alive.* Some of the guards here were once the wet towels you left on your bedroom floor. Others were the food you hid from your mothers in your messy rooms." She came closer to the children, "You aren't supposed to eat in your rooms, are you?" Diva laughed again at the horrified look on the children's faces.

"Oh, but you haven't heard the best part!" she cooed. "Some of these Guards are children who refused to take their baths," here she paused to lean over and poke Robert in the chest with her finger as she finished, *"or brush their teeth."*

But Robert surprised them all. Rather than being scared by the Tooth Fairy's poke or frightened by the Rot Guards, he gave a sharp battle cry and began to wipe his dirty boots on the floor. He scuffled his feet in a line of dirt and skid marks, then leapt up on the white couch and began to jump up and down.

"EEEEEAAAAHHHHHHH!!!!"   Diva

shrieked pointing to the floor.

Eva, Lauren, and Stubby gasped as they looked down at the very black footprints Robert's feet had trailed across the very white floor.

"What have you done? This room was just cleaned!! These floors are freshly whitened, polished and picked! Get down off of my couch this minute, you awful child!" the Tooth Fairy screamed.

"Well..." Robert said panting and giving her a smug smile, "how did you expect to keep all this white furniture and floors clean anyway? I mean, some dirt is *bound* to happen isn't it?" He crossed his arms across his chest, keeping his feet firmly on the couch.

"How did I expect to keep things *clean*?!" Diva screeched. "By flossing and brushing regularly, of course! Something you obviously do not appreciate, young man! GUARDS!" she yelled, turning a gaudy shade of purple.

At her command, the slimy, fuzzy mass of guards shuffled closer into the room.

"Take them to the Decaying Dungeon!" she shouted. At once, the rotting watchmen lurched over to surround the children. "Feed them nutritious food and make sure they brush and floss until those baby teeth come out! I *will* have the most exquisite baby teeth wishes! After that..." Diva paused again and took a few big breaths to calm herself down. "After that, they can have their stash of precious Halloween candy."

She moved toward the children, her white dress trailing behind her like a vapor. "You see, children, I will stick to my end of the deal... As a matter of fact, after *all* your baby teeth are out you can eat as much candy as you like in the Decaying Dungeon." She smoothed her gloves and sneered. "Oh, yes, you can eat it until your mouths rot and then the rest of you will rot as well. From the inside out! Then you'll beg to become members of my personal Rot Guard!" She whirled around to face the Guards, "Take them away!"

The children gasped in unison at this sudden turn of events, and Stubby let out a low moan, "Not the Decaying Dungeon! I won't go there again!" They heard a soft popping noise as he disappeared like a soap bubble.

"Run!" Eva directed, and the children began to dash about the room. Robert climbed over the top of the couch, knocking over a lamp. Lauren dashed toward the farthest corner while Eva ducked behind Diva and began to run circles around her.

"Stop them!" yelled the outraged Fairy. "Oh! Don't climb on the furniture with those dirty hands and feet! You there – grab that rodent! She's ruining my carpet!" She wrung her hands and wailed, "Ohh! Capture them, already!"

The Guard's hands were gooey, and the children were quick, but eventually Diva stood in the middle of the curvy room and yelled the ultimate magic word: "Freeze!"

Everyone in the room stopped moving at once. *"What has happened to us? I can't move at all!"* Eva thought in a panic as she struggled to try and move her frozen legs.

Diva sniffed and gave a little nod. She had used some of her fairy land magic to capture them.

With a huff, Diva pointed to the Captain of the Guard, releasing him from her freeze so he could rope each of the children's hands together with floss and present them to the fuming Fairy.

"I wouldn't normally use my precious magic for such ridiculous behavior," Diva said with a smirk, "but I suppose it's acceptable given our little deal." She leaned down and pointed at each of the children to unfreeze their rigid limbs.

"Let us go!" Eva demanded. "We only came here to get back the candy you stole! You had no right to take it!"

"What?" Diva gasped, spinning around from

her inspection of the now-trampled room to face the children. "I did you a favor by taking that candy. I take one small step in preventing tooth decay and this is how you thank me? Well! I am going to teach you some *long* overdue manners. While you are a guest in my home, perhaps I shall have you clean up the mess you made while I wait for those baby teeth to fall out. And don't even think about backing out on our little contract, my dears. There are far worse things than giving your baby teeth to me and becoming a member of my Guard... *Far worse things!*"

She stood back and examined the tips of her gloves. "Captain Rot, take them away."

Captain Rot, who was bigger than all the other guards and wore gold bars on the shoulders of his uniform, stepped forward and saluted Diva. From the putrid smell of him, Eva thought the captain might have been one of those children who refused to take a bath or brush his teeth.

The children squealed as slimy hands grabbed

their floss-tied arms and began to drag them from the room. "You're a wicked Tooth Fairy and I'm not going to give you my baby teeth!" Lauren cried as they were hauled out of the room kicking and *eewwwing*.

The doors slammed to the sound of Diva's indignant gasp.

8. Decaying Dungeon

The Rot Guards pulled the children down the hall past a number of newly-refinished, glistening white chambers. Eva gasped when they were suddenly herded past a room with lovely French doors. The plaque over the door read "Crown Room," but this room did not hold a collection of royal crowns, as one might think (if "one" wasn't already in the Tooth Fairy's mansion). In a glance, Eva saw through the glass to the huge pile of candy in the center of the room. It reached so high she could not see the top. *Hmmm...* she thought, *This is a dental crown room! A room made from a dental crown doesn't rot like a real tooth, so this room is where she is keeping the stolen Halloween candy!* Her discovery was cut short as the guard tightened his hold on the rope and continued yanking her forward.

"Our candy!" Eva screamed, wiggling.

Not expecting such a sudden outburst, the guard lost his slippery grip on her arms and Eva dropped to the floor, rolling and tripping him. The other befuddled guards, who had stood stock still in front of them at the alarming sound of a child's screech, began toppling over in succession, which gave Robert the opportunity to twist himself free as well.

"Hurry, Robert!" Eva called, "Run into the Crown Room!" She rushed to the door and turned around so that her floss-tied hands could easily turn the door's handle. She barely had time to register that, of course, the point of locking doors was useless when ghostly guards could pass through walls anyway. An unlocked door certainly came in handy now, though, as she and her friends were very much *alive.* And very much *wanted to stay that way!*

Robert scrambled to his feet and raced toward the room, dodging and dancing, lifting his feet high trying to avoid the guards who had slipped and landed on the floor during the struggle. Several Rot Guards lunged toward him trying to catch him with their goopy hands, but Robert rushed past Eva through the open door, and launched himself into the pile of candy like it was a mound of autumn leaves. Soon he was rolling around and shoving candy into his pockets wherever his tied hands could reach, whooping with glee as he burrowed deeper into the mountain of candy.

Eva was about to follow his lead when she heard Captain Rot speak for the first time. "Stophhh!" he ordered in a wet voice, "I haphhh your pphhriend, and she will not make it to the dungeon if you do not come along quietly. Ppphhhh...." He fizzled and sputtered as if the air was escaping from extra crevices in his mouth. Drool bubbled from the corner of his fuzzy lips onto his chest, and Lauren was splattered with green slimy droplets.

Lauren whimpered, shaking her rope floss and leaning away from the captain.

"Oh *drat*!" Eva huffed, "Robert, stop! They have Lauren!" Robert squirmed on his back in the pile of candy, and Eva shouted again, "*Robert!*"

"I'm coming," he grumbled, dragging himself into a sitting position and getting to his feet with a frustrated grunt. He stalked out of the Crown Room and a Rot Guard slammed the door behind him. Robert winced at the loud bang, and guards grabbed the children and hustled them forward to face the Captain.

"What-thhhh, did you Phhhh-ink you were going to accomplish-phhh by that little act?" he asked spraying them with spittle.

The children tried to wipe their faces while they gagged in disgust.

"No dinner phhor you tonight because ophhh that!" He announced and spun around to lead them toward a decrepit, stained door.

"Seriously, I couldn't eat now anyway," Robert shot back. "Your disgusting breath has totally ruined my appetite."

The Captain said nothing, giving Robert the double stink-eye before opening the filthy door leading to a stairwell that descended into the moldering darkness.

When the door opened, the smell told them this was the stairwell that lead to the Decaying Dungeon... The odor reeked of gym shoes, wet dogs and rotten eggs.

"Nooo!" Lauren cried, gagging. They all began to struggle harder against their captors but this time the guards were prepared and held tight to the floss around their wrists.

"Everyone-phhh seems to do that once the door to the Dungeon is open... I don't-phhh know why." Captian Rot laughed. "I phhink it smells quite nice down here, don't you boys?" The Rot Guards laughed with him as they pulled the children down the stairwell.

A green glow emanated from the walls of the Dungeon below. As the children descended, they saw the roots of Diva's castle were woven into a tight net of bars. Some of the roots had been broken away and hinges had been attached to allow for a dungeon door. The floor was a springy mat of green mold and flat stones and the walls seemed to be oozing something.

Captain Rot opened the Dungeon door and each of the children's guards removed the floss from their wrists and shoved them into the cell. The Captain closed and re-locked the cell door.

"I will return later phhhor your first lesson in mannner-phhs," he advised with a curl of his upper lip. Then he and the guards marched back up the stairs and clanged the door behind them.

"Ohhh... I think I'm gonna barf!" Lauren moaned. She was standing on tiptoes trying not to touch anything with any part of her body. "Gah! The smell!" she plugged her nose. "What are we going to do? We have to get out of here!"

9. Breaking Out

"Okay, don't panic," Eva soothed her friend as she paced. Eva hugged herself, trying to avoid touching the walls. Robert was the only one who didn't seemed to be bothered at all by the Decaying Dungeon. In fact, Robert had a small grin on his face as he quietly watched his friends talk.

Eva stroked her chin for a moment, and stopped pacing. She narrowed her eyes at Robert before she too began to grin. They both turned to Lauren with the same delighted look of mischief.

"Lauren," Robert asked calmly, "what did the Tooth Fairy say in our note about what candy can do to teeth if they aren't brushed?"

"Wait! Sugar!" Lauren cried, suddenly realizing what they were grinning about. "Oh my gosh! Candy will rot the bars because they're made of teeth!" Despite her happy discovery, she shuddered at the thought.

"There is no jail solid enough to hold these Junior Detectives!" Robert grinned and pulled out some of the Halloween candy he'd crammed into his pockets in the Crown Room. The three friends giggled and gave each other high fives and soft shoulder punches (being careful not to knock each other into any slimy walls).

They divided up Robert's impressive haul and applied the largest, stickiest pieces to the bars – which sizzled when the candy was applied and melted more quickly than Eva had expected. It shouldn't have come as a surprise, though, because the rotting smell of the Dungeon suggested the roots had been decaying for quite a while on their own.

"You'd think Diva would have taken care of the foundation of her house before fixing the rooms upstairs!" Lauren said.

"Oh no," Eva countered. "I'm going to guess Diva is *all* about looks from the way she reacted to Robert making a mess of her clean room. 'If it looks good to others, who cares what it's like where it can't be seen.'" The children agreed, and continued their work.

Carmel candies seemed to work best. They hissed as they stuck to the tooth roots, popping and steaming until the bars just shriveled and disappeared. The remainder of the candy dropped to the floor and began to bubble there.

Very quickly they had worked a section of the tooth bars away and were each able to squeeze through to the other side.

"You are just brilliant, Robert." Eva said, silently forgiving him for the stolen leaf jump.

"I can't stand this place any longer. Let's get out of here," Lauren whispered holding her nose.

"Agreed! Let's try to get to the Crown Room again. I have an idea." Eva turned and quietly began to tiptoe on the springy stones of the green floor toward the stairwell. The moldy floor and steps made it hard for the children to walk steadily, but holding on to the stairwell banister for balance was not an appealing thought, so they made their way cautiously.

Eva listened at the door to see if she could hear any guards outside. When she heard nothing, she slowly cracked the door open and peeked out. Captain Rot seemed very confident that they would not escape the Dungeon because he had not posted a guard!

Eva quickly scanned the hallway. It was also empty, so she gave her friends the signal with a wave of her hand and they each silently crept out and headed down the hall toward The Crown Room.

Despite the enormity of the Tooth Castle, they had no trouble re-tracing their path back to The Crown Room. When they got to the door,

Eva quietly opened it and ushered her friends inside before shutting the door behind them.

"Ohhh, it smells like candy in here!" Lauren exclaimed with a happy sigh, her nose still a bit red from pinching it so tightly against the horrible Dungeon smell. "Okay, now what's your idea?" she asked turning away from Robert, who was already searching the candy for his favorites.

"I'll show you," Eva answered. "Stubby!" she called out in a demanding whisper. "Stubby, I know you can hear me!" she called again.

Each of the children stood quietly waiting, holding their breath and listening.

Nothing.

"Stubby," Eva said in the best imitation of her mother's 'don't make me count to three' voice. Suddenly there was a soft popping noise.

"Ahhh... Geeze!" the ghost moaned appearing in the room. But his moan quickly turned to delight as he began looking around. "Ohhh! Look at all this Halloween candy!

Where did it come from?" he asked turning to Eva.

"This is the stolen Halloween candy, Stubby," Eva answered. "You knew about this because you told us that Diva was the one who took it."

He stared at her. "But, she told me that the Halloween candy had already been *spent* for the house remodel!" Stubby looked at the room full of candy, his eyes hungry.

But in the next moment, to the children's surprise, Stubby slowly began turning a gentle shade of red. His expression, which started as confused, became annoyed and then changed to really perturbed.

"She told me she was letting me go because she couldn't afford to pay me any longer!" Stubby huffed as little puffs of pink steam began to rise from his ghostly head.

"She threw me out in the cold and she hasn't even given me the letter of recommendation she promised!" The children began backing away as Stubby grew larger and redder with each angry word.

"I believed her... I dedicated myself to her for a full year. I felt sorry for her *'bad situation!'*" Stubby shouted, growing bigger and bigger until his entire ghostly belly surrounded the vast pile of Halloween candy in the Crown Room.

Eva shouted, "Hang on, you guys! I think we can make it home the same way we came in!" She gave each of them a quick shove toward Stubby until they lay on the piles of candy within his enlarged mass and held their breath, waiting to be transported back through the twisting Halloween vine to their homes.

Just then the door opened. "That will be enough of that, I think," Diva said and stalked in.

10. Not So Fast!

Stubby expelled his belly like a giant balloon releasing its gas. He whined and whistled as he shrunk, until at last he lay on top of the tallest pile of candy panting, his arms flung out beside him, exhausted. All of the ghostly chubbiness he once had seemed to have melted away leaving a tired, thin version of the ghost.

"Stubby?   Are you okay?" Eva asked, climbing the pile to reach him.

"I'm fine," he panted in a weak voice. "But she took all of my ghostly gas." Wheezing, he turned to Diva, and with as much energy as he could muster asked, "What have you done?"

"Well I took the candy, of course!" she replied crossing her arms on her chest. "How dare you try to betray me and take the candy back to their world! Good luck trying to get your former figure back!" She took a deep breath and blew on Stubby. And with just that little puff of her breath, he faded away like mist evaporating in the wind.

The last thing the children heard was a soft, moaning whisper, "Save some of your Halloween candy for when your dear friend Stub comes to visit?"

"No! Stubby!" Lauren cried. She was long past her fear of him and did not want to see him disappear. He was a friend and their only hope to get back home.

"And you! How did you get out of my Dungeon?" Diva demanded spinning around and grabbing Eva by the front of her shirt and shaking her.

"Stop it! Stop it!" Lauren cried rushing toward her friend. She flung her body at Diva, and suddenly froze in mid-air, her hair standing up like it was held by static electricity. The utter shock on her face made Diva snort with laughter.

"Heroic effort, dearie," Diva said, her steely finger pointed squarely at the suspended girl, "but you didn't think I could see that coming?" With her free hand, she lifted Eva slightly off the ground, dropping her in a heap beside Robert, and then pointed at both of them.

"But! But! You didn't even say freeze!" Robert cried. "That's against the rules!"

"The rules, he says!" Diva cackled for a long

moment then wiped an invisible tear from the corner of her glinting eye. "Oh, I needed a good laugh..." she sighed and Robert grimaced. "This is my house, and in my house, we follow my rules!"

"Geesh, how many times have I heard *that* from my parents..." Robert whispered from the corner of his mouth.

"And here is another rule, children: I want *pristine* baby teeth, so you *will* stay down in the Dungeon and brush your teeth until I have them all collected! Guards!" Diva shrieked.

"Why are you doing this to us?" Eva asked. "Why did you steal from kids just to get more for yourself?"

"Why?" Diva said with amazement. "*Why*, you ask? Because I deserve more!" She spat each word. "I work so hard collecting all of that magic, and *our* world gets hardly any of it any more. I am certain you had no idea that almost all of it is contracted out to *your* greedy world so you can make metal fly or watch silly pictures in some kind of glorified box. Most of your world doesn't even know you're using magic every day! So many of you don't even believe in it! There is no 'thank you' to fairies for collecting and *giving away* all of the magic that makes your world so happy... Nooo, you just want more and more and *more* for your precious video games or your fancy little cell phones. Who do you *really* think the greedy ones are here? You are all little piglets eating up the magic supply!" She finished huffing and glaring at the children.

The children stared at Diva until Eva said, "I may not know all about the magical world yet but I do know that there is no excuse for stealing."

"Missssstressphhh?" Captain Rot entered the room suddenly.

"Ah, my dear Captain," Diva said looking at her elegant wrist watch and choosing to ignore Eva's comment. "So nice of you to finally join us. Perhaps you could explain to me how the children got out of the Decaying

Dungeon and into the Crown Room. *Once again.*"

"I...Phhhhht...Uhhh," the Captain began.

"This will be your last chance to watch these children, Captain," she interrupted his sputtering. "Do I make myself crystal clear? Your... last... chance." With a wave of her hand Captain Rot began to melt.

"Phfffttt!" he cried as his fuzzy limbs began to pool at his feet. He shrunk into a brown, melting mass and made an attempt to swing his arms out toward Diva, but she only laughed and stepped farther away as the puddle expanded at her feet, bubbling and popping.

"Oopsie. I guess I didn't make myself clear," she smiled. "That *was* your last chance. Guards!" she yelled again.

Another Rot Guard (this one had a decaying pizza face) entered the room and paused to look at the brown and green slimy puddle on the floor. "Missstresss?" he drooled.

"Congratulations, you have been promoted to Captain." A soft 'puff' came from guard's shoulders and they could see the uniform now sported gold bars. "Take these children back to the Decaying Dungeon and make sure their teeth are brushed.   And *flossed,* for goodness sake!"

Diva turned to the children, "If you're going to try backing out on our deal and not offering me your baby teeth, I'm sure you'll see there are far worse punishments than becoming a Rot Guard." She nodded at the puddle of green goo. An eyeball had not yet melted and it rolled in the slime to turn and look slowly at the children as if to say *don't let this happen to you.*

11. A Good Idea

In the Decaying Dungeon, Eva paced the floor. Diva had assured the newly-appointed Captain that if any more candy was discovered missing from the Crown Room, he would go the way of his predecessor, so the children were particularly disheveled after a thorough frisking.

As she paced, Eva watched Lauren delicately smooth and re-smooth her clothing. Even Robert, who was inspecting the now reinforced tooth bars for cracks, seemed glum. "I don't know how she did it," he said, "but these things have some kind of fillings or something now." He looked up at his friends. "Even if we *did* have any candy, it wouldn't work on this stuff," he rapped his knuckles against the bars and the sound of their clanking echoed throughout the Dungeon.

Above them, Eva heard a Rot Guard pacing as well. Word had spread about the demise of their former Captain, and every precaution was being taken to earn Diva's favor.

Eva walked and listened and tapped her chin. Dental floss, toothbrushes and toothpaste sat in a pile, refused by the children. She knew it was only a matter of time before they'd be frozen again and the Rot Guard would attend to each of their teeth without their consent. The very thought made Eva's skin crawl.

"Eva, do you think your Mom could hear us if we called to her?" Lauren asked.

After trying to be so brave for what seemed like months in Fairy Land (though it was only hours), Eva finally looked on the verge of tears. "I tried that already," she replied softly,

"It didn't work... But she *will* come looking for us if I'm not back before dark, so don't worry."

Lauren moved to comfort her friend. "And thanks for trying to save me from Diva," Eva said, putting her hand in Lauren's.

"You would have done the same for me," Lauren shrugged.

A loud clang caused the girls to jump. Robert was now on the floor using his feet to kick the tooth bars in an effort to see if one would break.

"Heyyphhhfff!" The guard at the top of the stairs opened the door and shouted down at Robert, "Sttoooppphh that or I will come down there and make you stoppphhh!"

"Whatever!" Robert grumbled and stopped kicking. "Hey! We've been down here *forever*! When can we get a snack or something?" Robert yelled up to the Guard.

When they heard nothing, Lauren assured him, "It was a good idea Robert."

"Hey, Robert," Eva turned to him, "Do you think we could use the dental floss to cut the bars?" She ran to the pile and tossed aside the tooth brushes and paste to pull out a tube of floss.

"I don't know Eva," he replied, "they seem pretty solid now."

"Oh!" Lauren said sitting up taller and pointing at the dental floss. "Floss! It's like string!"

"Yeah?" Eva said turning back to Lauren "So?"

"Well, you and Robert both have loose teeth." Lauren said standing up and moving nearer so she could speak more quietly, "My parents once helped me get a loose tooth out by tying a string to my tooth and the other end to a door. They slammed the door when I was ready – and I didn't even feel it! My tooth just popped right out."

"Yeah!" Robert smiled. "I get it! We could use the baby tooth to make our *own* wish once it's out."

"Yes!" Lauren agreed. "No one said we couldn't use the wish *ourselves* since we're in Fairy Land..."

"Lauren!" Eva interrupted. "You're brilliant!" She patted her friend on the back. "I can't believe we didn't think of it sooner."

"Thanks," Lauren smiled, "So who's tooth is it gonna be?"

"We can use mine." Robert volunteered, wiggling one of his lower front teeth. "I've been wiggling it with my tongue so it's pretty loose now."

"Cool! Thanks!" Eva grinned. "Open your mouth and hold still for a sec and I'll tie the floss around it."

After a couple of slippery tries the children were ready. They tied the other end of floss to a bar and planned to give Robert a little shove since they didn't have a door to slam.

"Ok," Lauren whispered, "On the count of

three. One... Two... Three!"

Eva pushed Robert with as much strength as she could and he fell backward to the floor, his hands reaching for his mouth.

"Owwww!" he cried, "I thought you said it didn't hurt."

"I meant it didn't hurt your *tooth*! Not your rear end! Sorry, Robert. Are you okay?"

"Yeah," he replied, feeling the empty spot in his gums with his tongue.

"Guys, look!" Eva said pointing to the floor where Robert's tooth now lay. The tooth sparkled on the stone floor like gleaming gold and was glowing from within. As the children paused, they could almost hear the powerful, calming hum that radiated from it.

"Wow! Is that my tooth?" Robert asked crawling toward it.

"No, young man," Diva said from the top of the stairwell, "That is *my* tooth!"

Robert lunged for the tooth but before he

could grab it, Diva appeared in front of him in a burst of glitter and reached down to nab the tooth herself.

"You silly children thought that a baby tooth could come out in *my* house and I wouldn't know about it? How many times do I have to tell you I am a Tooth Fairy! This is what we *do*!"

"That's *my* tooth!" Robert yelled, and dove to make another grab for it.

"Excuse me?" she asked, holding the tooth away from him. "I don't think I heard you correctly. Did you say you wanted your friends to be flossed by the Rot Guards?"

12. Daylight

Guards began filing into the cell, forming circles around the girls. Eva looked to Lauren, who stood trembling. Then she looked around hoping for an idea, but there was nothing left to do, so Eva did the only thing she could think of. With a desperate leap at the closest Guard, she tried to create a diversion.

"Bounces off me and sticks to yooooou!" she shrieked and jumped onto the Guard. He flung out his hands to stop her but it was too late. He was kicking and whirling around, in an effort to detach the ferocious child from his leg but Eva held on like a rodeo champ. The other Guards stood uneasily for a moment, looking back and forth from Diva then to Lauren then to the watchman under attack. Fists were flying and feet were kicking. No one was sure who was wailing, but at last the Guard flung Eva to the ground.

"Sssshhhhee pinched me...phhhttt!" the Guard howled.

"Oh!" Eva softly cried as she lifted her head. The fall had jarred her whole body and she saw, with some surprise, her own loose tooth had been knocked out and was laying on the floor, glowing, in front of her. Before the Guard could grab her arms again, she reached forward to scoop it up and hide it in her clenched fist.

Empowered by the magical wish she now clutched, Eva hissed at the Guard, "Don't touch me!"

Robert dropped his arms in defeat after he saw that Eva had been grabbed by the guard again. "No... I..." he sputtered. Diva's smile spread slowly as she closed her hand in a fist around Robert's baby tooth. She had felt a small tingle of something that could only be described as *electricity* when the Rot Guard knocked Eva to the ground, however, Diva assumed it was from the young man's tooth since it pulsed with magic and she was even more eager to use the power.

"Robert, wait!" Eva yelled. But the Guard reached forward, smacking her with his slimy hand, and she fell to the ground again, dropping her tooth into a crack in the brick floor. With dismay, Eva felt the magic leave her hand and she knew that she and her friends were never going to leave this cell.

"Wait! Wait!" Robert cried out after seeing Eva struck. "I do want to give you my tooth, Diva! Just don't hurt my friends!"

"Why thank you." Diva nodded and acknowledged the gift. She opened her fist to study the prize glowing in her palm, "Hmph, this doesn't have as much wish power as it *could* have had if you'd left it in longer, but I suppose it'll be enough to finish my home renovations before the ball is over tonight."

"Not so fast!" Lauren cried.

Everyone froze – without the magic words – and stared at the plump little girl with her fist in the air. "It just so happens that I have a perfectly good wish to make myself!" Shimmers of glowing light leaked from her clenched hand, and her eyes were like hot diamonds.

"What?" Diva screeched, gaping at Lauren's raised fist. "How did you... Where did you get that?" She turned her scrutiny to Robert's weakly glowing tooth in her own hand. "Give me that other tooth!"

But Lauren shook her head and glared at Diva as she yelled out, "I wish my friends and I were back in the basement of Eva's house with all of the Halloween candy!" Lauren paused and then quickly added. "And I wish for a new bike for Robert!"

"We had a deal!" the Tooth Fairy screamed over a strange wind which had begun to blow through the cell like a tornado.

The children heard a familiar whoosh and a thunderous crack. Lauren's fist dropped and Robert looked around wildly. Only Eva ran toward the hole which had now opened in the air, sucking candy from the room like a giant vacuum hose.

"You guys!" she shouted over the Tooth Fairy's shrieks.

With a large "BOOM!" the children found themselves pulled upwards and tumbling around and around with hoards of candy enveloping them. The experience felt something like being tumbled around in your laundry dryer with 100 bags of candy - except there was no hot air. No matter how much you love candy *no one* wants to experience it this way.

"I will not forget this!" the Tooth Fairy

shrieked over the din. Her voice was far below them, growing weaker as they tumbled upward.

Eva dared to squint one eye open and then she saw it: The Tooth Fairy's clawed hand reached up through the tunnel and made one last grab for the children's ankles. Desperately, Eva kicked at candy and thrashed against the current of the Halloween vine, she feared, that they would be captured again and free fall with all of the candy back down into the Decaying Dungeon.

She kicked her foot and felt it land solidly upon Diva's outstretched hand. The Tooth fairy made one last scream in pain and pulled her hand from the candy tornado. The vine closed and they all picked up speed for a bit twirling through the green and orange vine tunnel.

Robert 'whooped' and hollered his enjoyment in the ride but it didn't take long before the wind from the candy roller coaster began to die down, and soon they felt themselves falling, no longer pulled upward by the wind.

"Oh noooo! We're falling!" Eva cried out.

A blast of cold air hit them as the tunnel opened up again and they were dumped, ungracefully, onto a mountain of taffy, jelly beans and chocolate bars. The children 'ooofed' and 'ouched' as they rolled onto the candy pile, and just when they thought they had landed safely, the rest of the candy from the tunnel came raining down and buried them as it fell.

When it finally stopped, Eva lay quietly trying not to cry but it was no use. When the last caramel dropped in the utter silence, she broke into sobs and wailed like a baby. It was completely unprofessional and Robert would surely try to revoke her Junior Detective status, but she could hold it in no longer. *We are still in the dungeon!* She thought to herself. *Only now we will never get out.*

13. We Might As Well Eat It...

Eva hiccupped and sniffed. It was so nice and dark under the pile, and the candy smelled so lovely. She wriggled her way further down, knowing that she didn't have the strength to fight the Rot Guards, but not wanting to make it easy for them either. What a shame all these treats would all be taken away when the Rot Guards dug them out. If she hadn't already been crying, she'd have started now.

When hands began clawing at the wrappers, shoveling candy aside and reaching into the darkness for her, she shrunk down further.

"You're gonna have to come get me!" she shouted using her hands to try and dig down further into the pile like a mole.

"I'm trying to!   Geesh!" she heard from above.

"Lauren?" Eva stopped burrowing.

"Yes!" she shouted.   "Where *are* you?" Lauren's hands were scratched by the wrappers and she was acutely aware that her grass-stained pants were now also covered in chocolate. "I can tell you one thing: I am going to burn this outfit when I get home," she said.

Daylight began to shine in mottled patches and soon Eva could see her friend's disgusted face. "I swear, this has been the grossest day ever."

"Lauren?" Eva said again.

"The one and only," Lauren said, reaching through the shifting candy and grabbing Eva's hand. "Help me out a little, here," she said.

Eva began treading candy, propelling herself upward with as much force as she could, laughing and shouting. "We're home? Lauren? Robert?"

"Robert! Robert, where are you?" Lauren called as Eva began to pull herself out of the heap. "Robert!" Lauren dropped to her knees and began to dig through bite-sized candy bars, bags of sour gummies and licorice.

"I'm over here," he mumbled, shaking his head out of the candy pile and waving one hand. He seemed to be trying to open a chocolate crunch bar with his teeth.

"Geeze, Robert. How can you eat that after we saw what the candy did to those tooth roots in the Dungeon?" Lauren asked pulling his arm to help free him.

"Well, I'll brush and floss more often that's for sure! Besides..." he added with a grin, "we should get started as soon as possible on this candy. How else are we gonna finish it before next Halloween?"

"Oh you're not going to eat all of this candy," a familiar voice said from the stairwell.

"Mom?" Eva exclaimed. "We're home! We're really here!" She turned and hugged her friend. "You did it, Lauren! You wished us all back!"

"And a bike! Thank, you Lauren!" Robert whooped, spotting the gift and rushing over to inspect his new wheels.

"But how did you do it?" Eva asked. "How did you know I lost my tooth?"

"I saw it on the ground when you fell," Lauren shrugged. "But then that Rot Guard smacked you and it rolled away. I saw that Diva was distracted by Robert's tooth, and the Guards were all looking at the pinch mark you left, and ... Well, no one was paying any attention to me, so I just..." she shrugged again, "grabbed it, I guess..."

"Woohoo! You saved us!" Eva shouted and hugged her friend harder.

"And I got a bike!" Robert said hopping up

and down. The girls turned to scowl at him. "What! I *did* get a bike."

"Ahemmm…" Mrs. O'Hare cleared her throat and stood on the steps frowning at the mounds of candy in her basement. "Children! This candy must be returned in good condition for the other kids in the neighborhood to enjoy!"

"Give it back?" Robert looked at Mrs. O'Hare, momentarily distracted from his bike. "Look at all this loot! We couldn't have collected this much candy if we had been able to trick-or-treat for a week!"

The friends paused to look at one another and then began doing a little happy dance. Eva and Lauren locked arms and jigged as Robert laid his bike down in a pile and began rolling around, tossing candy in the air and letting it rain down on him like they had found gold at the end of the rainbow.

It wasn't long however before their little celebration was interrupted again by a loud, "Excuse me…" Mrs. O'Hare looked disappointed. "I don't think you really mean to keep all of this." She stood on the bottom step and crossed her arms.

"Mom!" Eva exclaimed, stopping her dance with Lauren so quickly that they both fell down.

"Mom, we found the Halloween candy! It was stolen by our neighborhood TOOTH FAIRY and we got it back using my tooth as a wish!" Eva exclaimed, sitting up and pointing to the new hole in her smile.

"I can see that," Ms. O'Hare said looking around. "That sounds very creative and exciting. And you'll have to tell me all about it *after* you return this candy."

"But that'll take forever!" Robert complained.

"Wait - the Tooth Fairy!" Eva said, suddenly nervous. She stood up and looked at her friends. "When Diva finds out we're back home again she'll come looking for us! What do we do?"

"Hide the candy!" Robert bayed, immediately

shoving candy down the front of his sweatshirt in fistfuls. Lauren began to mound piles toward her.

"Children, stop," Mrs. O'Hare commanded in the stern tone Eva had tried to copy when she'd summoned Stubby in the Crown Room. The effect was immediate, as they all stopped and turned to look at Eva's mom.

"There's no need to worry about Diva. She can't make it here without help from the Tooth Corporation. I've spoken to the Board and they've temporarily taken away the sparkle that allows her to fly. When they find her, there will be a trial for the Halloween candy she took." She shook her head and rubbed her temples as if a slight headache was beginning to form. "Technically that is all they can charge her with at the moment. Now, about this candy..."

"You've spoken to the Board?" Lauren's eyes grew wide. She looked toward Robert and Eva. "But, but... Diva was going to keep us in her Dungeon and turn us into one of her Rot

Guards! Can't she be charged with kid rotting or something?"

"Yeah!" Robert added. "How did you speak to the Board? How long were we gone?"

"Ahhh, Robert," Mrs. O'Hare suppressed a laugh and turned to Lauren. "Lauren, dear, you didn't become Rot Guards, now, did you?" Her tone was gentle. "Of course, you *could* all use a bath and a good tooth scrubbing, but you haven't actually begun to rot... Yet."

"Well, I, for one, am not giving this stash to anyone. We're the ones who risked our lives to get it back!" Robert sputtered. He immediately regretted his outburst, blushing bright red as Mrs. O'Hare raised an eyebrow at him.

Eva knew that look all too well. "But mom, *look* at all of this. How would we ever get this much candy back to all the kids it was stolen from? It's impossible. We might as well eat it...." she trailed, peeking at her Mom through her lashes.

Mrs. O'Hare sighed and took a seat on the step. "Children, this morning you all felt terrible because someone had taken your candy." She paused and they each nodded at her. "How do you think all of the children who are still missing their candy feel right now?"

"I know Brandon and Jenna felt really bad when I talked to them on the phone..." Lauren said quietly.

"I'm sure. And aren't they your friends?" Mrs. O'Hare continued gazing at the three of them, pausing thoughtfully before speaking again. "I know you didn't take the candy in the first place, but wouldn't it seem like you were stealing it all over again if you didn't give it back?"

The children dropped their eyes and were quiet. Robert kicked at a few stray wrappers and Lauren sighed. Eva was the first to reply. "You're right, Mom. I guess we just got excited..." She looked at her friends who slowly nodded their agreement.

Robert began to pull candy from underneath his sweat shirt and Lauren said, "Well, since you put it that way…"

"There's just so much of it, mom. How do we get it all back to the other kids?"

"Ah, my darlings," Mrs. O'Hare smiled and stood up from where she had previously been sitting on the step. "You're not lucky enough to keep all of this candy for yourselves, but I have a few friends that *are* lucky, and they just might be able to help you out. If you can convince them, that is."

"I don't understand," Eva said giving her mom a quizzical look.

Mrs. O'Hare reached her arms out and pulled Eva toward her in a big hug. "Someday we'll have to sit down and have a little chat about… well… about this kind of thing. But for now, why don't you all leave the candy here and come upstairs with me." Mrs. O'Hare winked at them. "I'll fix you each a cup of hot cocoa and help get you started on your next adventure to return this Halloween hoard."

Then Mrs. O'Hare patted Eva's cheek and turned to walk up the stairwell.

"Okay," Eva said, "but first I want to pick up my room a little bit. I think I've left some things on the floor for a while..."

"Yes," Lauren said looking down at herself. "Can we work out how to return all the candy tomorrow? I want to go home and clean up first."

"Yeah, me too," Robert agreed.

"I think that's a great idea," Mrs. O'Hare agreed with a nod and smiled. "We wouldn't want to add any new recruits to the Rot Guard now, would we...?"

The End

This ends Book 1 of the Magical Mystery Series: Case of the Halloween Heist.

We hope you enjoyed Eva, Lauren and Robert's first adventure in the Magical Mystery Series!

Please come and visit us at our website www.magicalmysteryseries.com for more information about the authors and illustrator.

While visiting the site please enjoy a sneak peak of the next two books!

Coming in 2013!

A Magical Mystery Book 2: The Case of Finding a Leprechaun's Luck

Lauren has been kidnapped by the former Tooth Fairy, Diva, and it's up to her friends to save her! Our heroes, Eva and Robert, must win a prestigious tournament in Leprechaun Land to earn magical wishing coins and defeat Diva once more.

A Magical Mystery Book 3: The Case of the Christmas Crime

In order to ensure the safety of Christmas and return the stolen magic, our heroes must once again battle Diva (and her Mom?!) to defeat the Snow Empire's evil plan.

Will our heroes be able to follow the clues and save the day while battling the abominable snowman and befriending an enslaved dragon?... all before their curfew?

Made in the USA
Charleston, SC
02 October 2013